Bertram Bear and the Rivals

Published by Mithra Publishing 2019.

This is a work of fiction. Names, characters, businesses, places, events, locales, and incidents are either the products of the author's imagination or used in a fictitious manner. Any resemblance to actual persons, living or dead, or actual events is purely coincidental.

Copyright © Gregory Gower 2019

Best Dishes
Gregory Gower

About the author

Gregory Gower was born in 1935 – so growing up and schooling were mixed with a world in turmoil. Most persons have the luxury of not experiencing bombs being dropped on them. He was four years of age when the war started and ten when it ended. Many days and nights were spent in an air raid shelter having to cope with listening to a gun emplacement nearby firing at enemy aircraft who were dropping their deadly cargo over Kent.

A noise so loud you would have thought your ears would have burst. His house had a direct hit and he was still in bed fast asleep when the curtains and the foot of his bed caught alight and he was rescued by a A.R.P. Warden! Many houses were destroyed and damaged later when the first of the many doodlebugs dived into the road.

He managed to gain his 11 plus at the age of 13. He went to Westwood Secondary Modern School then onto Dartford Grammar School. First job was training as a Compositor in Posners, Walters and Harrisons, Shoe Lane, Fleet Street. Second job was with Jones and Darke Rubber Plantation Office in Fenchurch Street.

He joined the Royal Air Force in 1953. Was sent abroad and served in Aden where experienced active service. Five months later he was posted to a Fighter Station/Staging Post at Sharjah where he served out the remainder of his service. On leaving the Royal Air Force, he became a Civil Servant and worked in the Passport Office and then transferred to 13 Downing Street in the United Nations Department.

Became seriously ill in 1960 and ended up in the Neurological Ward at Brooke Hospital – not expected to live!

In 1976 met Brenda and after a short engagement, married her in 1977. They have one Ginger cat called Josie who brings in leaves and feathers, but no mice – yet!

He is an acting/singing member and Vice Chairman of Eastbourne Gilbert and Sullivan Society. He is editor for NODA National Operatic & Dramatic Association News Magazine for South East England. A columnist for an on-line Newspaper – thesussexnewspaper.com Read the GG Column. Also Columnist for www.theuknewspaper.co.uk Speaker's Corner. A collection Secretary for N.C.H. Action for Children Charity in Eastbourne and is a member of Emmanuel Church Choir.

Visit www.bookworm.org.uk

Other books by the same author:

Picture Poetry Painting Book
Derbyshire Reflections & Others) Poetry, Prose
With Mixed Feelings) & Goodness Knows
Food For Thought   Poetry, Prose & Recipes

A Touch of Heaven & Other Short Stories
I Remember it Well & other Short Stories
Christmas is Coming Short Stories & Sketches
Mistaken Identity
A Joyride to Murder & The Steal
The Christmas Tree Story   Illustrations by Amanda Breach
The Adventures of Bertram Bear   Illustrations by Amanda Breach
Bertram Bear and the Rivals Illustrations by Mira Homer

In the Pipeline
A Baker's Dozen & Another Baker's Dozen
A Sequel to Murder
TIME A Sci-fi with three endings

Bertram Bear Rules Illustrations by Mira Homer
Bertram Bear and the Ginger Cat Illustrations by Mira Homer
Bertram Bear Goes on Holiday Illustrations by Mira Homer
Bertram Bear in Pantomime Illustrations by Mira Homer

Future projects
Rhyme & Reason Poetry & Prose - some new, some old
Letters to Nobody
Hidden Agenda
Stranglehold – A Three Act Play
Enigma
Inspector Graves Investigates
The Treasure   Illustrations
It Can Happen in a Week

Bertram Bear's World
Bertram Bear and the Burglars

Bertram Bear Goes Back in Time
Bertram Bear Visits the Toy Shop
Bertram Bear Finds Buried Treasure
Bertram Bear Goes Hunting

Living With Hope - Autobiography

Bertram Bear and the Rivals

Mira Homer

Mira was born in the Czech Republic and studied drawing and graphics in Prague, before graduating in art and design from the University of Brighton. She is a keen documentary photographer and has travelled widely in Europe, Asia and Australasia.

She has worked in art education as well as professional craft, specialising in ceramics and wood, and has produced 3-D work and illustrations for a number of publications. She lives in East Sussex with her husband and three children.

mirahomer@hotmail.com

The Characters:

Linda & Tony Glover (Parents)
Henry Glover (their son)
Bertram Bear
Mitch Bear (Bertram's Friend)
Lookalike Bertram Bear
Thomas the Cat
George next door's Dog (Left side)
Bruce next door's Dog (Right side)
Pinch and Punch next door Cats (Right side)
Charlie the Hedgehog
Al the Owl
Peregrine
A Horrible Dog (Growler)
Three horrible Cats (Biff, Bash, & Butt)

Bertram Bear and the Rivals

Chapter 1 Moving In

Great excitement as new neighbours were at last going to occupy two houses that had been empty for a couple of years. The house next to Henry and his family and the house two plots away on the same side. It seemed that families that had been together in their other houses and moved en bloc to Coombes corner of the world. Linda and Tony Glover had been living in this quiet cul-de-sac for almost eleven years. Their son, Henry had been very ill with a mysterious complaint that needed a doctor's visit and medicine.

Moving in went swimmingly and both families seemed to be very friendly until the next day when the pets arrived. There were going to be two cats and one large Alsatian called Bruce. Thomas didn't know the name of the two cats as nobody had called them. Bruce dwarfed George and would be no match should there be a fight. As soon as George saw Bruce, he skedaddled to the rear of his kennel and no amount of persuasion from Thomas was he able to coerce George to appear, excepting when the owner called George for his supper he came out so fast he knocked Thomas over and disappeared through his dog door.

Thomas said, 'We won't see him again tonight Charlie.'

It was Charlie the Hedgehog that had crawled slowly into the garden looking for his customary saucer of milk. His eyes blinked at Thomas and he said very slowly which matched his walking speed.

'Any chance of some milk?'

'Oh where's my manners of course you can have some milk, you'll have to come to the kitchen, I hope you can manage a few more yards.'

'Yes! I think so. Can I have some bread with my milk and a little sugar, I like a little sugar, it's sort of comforting food and the nights are drawing in and it has certainly turned winterish.'

Thomas was wondering how he was going to ask his owner for the bread and sugar. He needn't have worried because his owner must have read Charlie's mind because she placed a warm bowl of milk with bread down for him.

'That's really nice.' he said to Thomas between laps 'and it's sweet as well.'

'I have the best owner's in the world.' said, Thomas.

Linda put down Thomas's supper. It was succulent chicken in jelly, one of his favourites followed by a bowl of water. Thomas wasn't keen on milk and it was just as well because if he had left it, it would have gone by the morning with Charlie around.

All thoughts of the very large dog next door to them had disappeared from Thomas's mind while he was eating. He couldn't eat for ever and after he had licked his lips about thirty times he said good night to Charlie who curled up in Thomas's bed. Thomas went off to find his Linda's lap. She had laid down on the settee and her husband Tony was sprawled on the other chair.

The television was not on but a coal fire was burning brightly and shadows appeared to be dancing around the walls and Thomas leapt effortless onto her lap and washed and washed himself to a frazzle as he was thinking of the enormous trouble that might lay ahead.

All of a sudden Thomas froze and although the lap of his owner was comfortable he had unwittingly forgot to tell Bertram of the new arrivals. He must go quickly to Henry's room. That's where Bertram spent most of his time now that other things had died down. Henry had to stay in bed for another three days and was awake most of the time and Bertram had that distant stare.

Thomas crept into the room and Henry had fallen asleep and Bertram and Mitch were playing cards on the shelf. Thomas looked up and sprang from the floor to Henry's bed and then leapt from the bed to the shelf. Bertram, Mitch and Thomas looked towards the bed as Henry stirred. It would be an awkward moment if Henry woke up as Bertram and Mitch were holding playing cards in their paws. Henry made a comforting noise and turned over. Thomas related the news to Bertram and all Bertram could say was 'Oh dear!'

Chapter 2 Back to School

Bertram and Mitch had to stay as toys while Henry was still resting from his illness. Coming alive during the night time was a bit boring as nothing really happened during that time.

The weekend came and went and Henry prepared himself for school, he wasn't really looking forward to going. But as Henry's mum had told him, he had to have the knowledge of doing things. Henry would stand and look at his mum and say 'What does knolige mean?'
Mum would say, 'If you go to school you will find out.'

As soon as Henry left the house and in the car and turned left out of the road on his way to school, Bertram and Mitch were down the stairs and outside in the garden. This was something new to them and Bertram realised that normally Henry would have to be asleep before the toys came alive and at first Bertram thought their secret had been breached and the whole world knew about them coming alive, but as it turned out all was not lost because whether Henry was asleep or out of sight they could do what they like.

George, Thomas, Bertram and Mitch were having a meeting on how to gauge Bruce and whether he was going to be a friend or foe.
Suddenly Bertram looked towards the dividing fence which was barely four feet high. He had heard scuffling noises and then a head appeared. It was Bruce and he barked three times and then he said, 'My name is Bruce, well it's what my master calls me.'

Bertram stood his ground and bared his chest as much as a bear could and asked if he was going to be friendly. Bruce thought for a moment. 'Well that could be difficult. I've been trained to look after property.'

George said, 'A guard-dog, oh my goodness, that's the last thing we need round here.'

Bruce said, 'Do you mind, I'm not a thing, I'm a dog – well I was when I last looked.'

Bertram, 'You had better apologise, George.'

'Sorry – I didn't mean to be rude.'

Bertram said 'What breed are you?'

'I'm an Alsatian,' said Bruce rather proudly.

George said, 'You're going to find the garden a bit small to run around in.'

Bruce said, 'No I shall be okay – next door to us they are going to knock down the fence.'

A distant voice called out, 'George, come on boy. It's time for your walk.'

George gave his excuses and left the group and scrambled under the fence – it was difficult as he knew he was putting on weight. I must run more often or eat less – perhaps not – I'm too set in my ways and I do love eating. George's hind legs seem to be working overtime as he went under the fence.

'Anyway,' said Bruce, 'It's Pinch and Punch you'll have to keep an eye on. They are the meanest cats you will ever find around here.'

Bertram said, 'Unusual names they have?'

'Yes and it suits their personalities – Pinch will steal anything that's not screwed down and Punch will hit you when your back is turned.'

'Oh dear.' said Thomas.

'Oh dear indeed.' said Bruce, 'Be careful they work as a team.'

Pinch was sunny himself on a mound of dirt. He had dug a huge hole and was laying in it as he liked the coolness of the earth on his back and the sun on his tummy. To look at him you wouldn't think butter would melt in his mouth. Punch was knocking the stuffing out an old woollen rabbit. He was doing his training getting ready for the next fight. They hadn't met next door's collection of pets yet and they hoped they would be a push over as rivalry over territory was vital to Pinch and Punch and too many cats in one area was bad news.

Little did they know the surprise they were going to get when they ventured beyond the fence, but they should have got an insight when the woollen rabbit got up and walked towards the fence in question and disappeared under it. Pinch and Punch stood with open mouths as the Rabbit passed them and said, 'I'm off next door.' He flopped around a bit as he was almost flat and when he was brand new he was nicely rounded. He really was the little boy's toy, but Pinch took it and gave it to Punch for a Birthday present

*   *   *   *

Henry came home from school and sighed rather heavily!

'I don't know!'

'What don't you know dear?'

'Whether I did the right thing by using my middle name, the teachers at school keep saying is it going to be Brian or Henry?'

'Well darling you wanted to change, because you said that Brian was old hat.'

'Well I suppose so!'

'I hope you are not thinking of changing it back again?'

'No I don't think so – it's just that when they call out the register, they say Henry Glover and I had forgotten I'd changed my name and they all stare at me waiting for me to say yes – I'm here.'

'Well darling you will just have to get used to it, because I'm calling you Henry.'

Chapter 3 The Meeting

Bertram cowered when he saw this apparition appear from under the fence, almost unrecognisable and there was no side to him – in fact he was flat as a pancake. He flopped down on the ground in front of Bertram and said, 'Hello, my name is Ronald.' Bertram managed to recover from the shock of seeing such a wreck.

Ronald said, 'I know what you are thinking – how did I become this miserable looking wretch?'

'Yes,' said, Bertram.

'I've been beaten by Punch – at one time I belonged to the young boy who lives next door and he took me out in the garden one day and forgot to take me back in the house and Punch took me away and placed me in a tree for three days and it rained for two of them.'

Mitch remarked, 'Oh you poor thing.'

'I'm not a thing, I'm a rabbit.'

'Well you don't look……..'

Bertram stopped Mitch from saying the rest of his sentence. Bertram turned to Thomas who had been looking on bemused and said, 'Perhaps you could take him inside and put him somewhere where he could get dried.'

Thomas picked up Ronald and took him inside the house and put him next to the settee, it was the nearest piece of furniture to the fire that was burning brightly.

*   *   *   *

'Did you see that?' said Punch.

Pinch said, 'How is it possible for you to talk?' Pinch put his paw up to his mouth and realised he was talking too. 'How is this possible?'

'Don't ask me.' said, Punch. 'There must be something in the air.'

* * * *

Had Pinch and Punch realised that they were in the boundary of Bertram Bear's circle and that the magic of animals talking was only because of his presence they probably wouldn't have started trying to take over the whole area and when Henry came home from school, things returned to normal and Bertram and Mitch made sure they were in Henry's bedroom.

It was the following morning after Henry went off to school that trouble began to brew as Punch and Pinch entered into the garden where Thomas was sunning himself under a watering sun – it was Punch that came along and kicked dirt into Thomas's face with his paws. He looked comical with his back to Thomas and digging a hole like mad.

Thomas got up and growled at Punch.

'Is that all you can do?' said Punch.

'No.'

'You want to have a fight?'

'No.'

'If you want to keep this garden you'll have to.'

Bertram Bear was witness to this assault on Thomas and Mitch said, 'Aren't you going to intervene.'

'No. Said, Bertram

'Why not?'

'Because if I do, Thomas would lose face and he wouldn't thank me.'

'But...but!'

'No Mitch I just couldn't do that.'

Mitch said, 'I thought you liked Thomas.'

'Of course I like him. What kind of question is that.'

'Well he will probably be thrashed within an inch of his nine lives.'

'Better for him to receive a bashing and he will know what to do next time.'

Mitch said, 'Remember what I looked like when George got hold of me, I don't want him to go through all that.'

'That was different.'

'How do you make that different?'

'It just is.'

The fight had begun while they argued. Punch didn't have it all his own way as Thomas as gentle as he was, managed to bite Punch's ear. Bertram and Mitch watched as Thomas limped towards the back door.

Bertram frowned, 'We will have to do something to stop those two coming into this garden.'

Mitch couldn't understand the reasoning behind the remarks of Bertram when he could have stopped the fight in the beginning.

Chapter 4 A Visit From George

His owner took Thomas off to get treatment and she spoke to him all the way there. She told him this was the place she took his friend the hedgehog. Thomas had his temperature taken and he felt that his dignity had been breached and hoped nobody was looking. He had an injection. He never felt that and his paw had been bandaged and saving Linda going back and forth he had to take some pills for three days and stay indoors.

Thomas's bed had been brought in from the kitchen and placed near the fire.

As there was so much activity in the house Bertram and Mitch had to stay in Henry's bedroom what with the owner roaming around the house. Bertram leaned out of the widow and saw George by his kennel and he spoke to him telling him what had happened that morning and it might be a good idea if he went to visit Thomas.

'Do you think his owner will let me in?'

'Take something along with you, you never know.'

George went into the house and there was a terrific noise and George came out with a bunch of flowers in his mouth. He scrambled under the fence and placed the flowers on the doorstep and barked three times.

He picked up the flowers.

As soon as the door opened he went in.

Linda didn't understand the meaning and anyway who had heard of a dog giving flowers to a cat. George placed the flowers on the kitchen floor and walked towards the lounge door and barked. Linda saw at last the significance and opened the door for him.

He wagged his tail and looked up at her and walked to where Thomas was in his cot.

He whispered to him, 'Bertram told me all about your trouble, so I have come to visit you and I brought you some flowers.'

'That's very kind of you.' whispered Thomas.

George settled down beside Thomas and they both looked like they were going to sleep. Henry's mum left the room. She was shaking her head in disbelief as she went out to put the flowers in a vase. She spoke her thoughts, 'I wonder where George got the flowers from?'

Chapter 5 Bruce

Bertram and Mitch hadn't seen Bruce at all the first week after the neighbours had moved in that last Saturday when he had poked his head over the fence. He said he was a trained guard dog, but they couldn't see what he had to guard, surely not the house.

Bertram and Mitch were still sitting on the shelf playing cards as Thomas was still grounded with a bad paw and it would be dangerous for Bertram and Mitch to visit him and if caught Linda and Tony might have a fit.

Outside there was this deep throaty bark and both Bertram and Mitch walked along the shelf to the window and saw Bruce leaning up against the fence.

He looked disappointed to find nobody there until Bertram shouted down to him and more or less related the events that had happened yesterday.

Bruce looked puzzled – how is it possible for you to speak, it is Saturday and Henry….

Bertram said, 'Henry has gone out for the day, something to do with a school outing. It's very quiet without him. When he gets boisterous I get flung across the room sometimes.'

'Do you think he might be looking for another toy to play with and getting fed up with you?'

'I don't know.'

'When I was a puppy everybody thought I was cute and cuddly I was loved by Michael the boy in the house. They didn't reckon on me becoming large so my master of the house trained me as a guard dog for his place of work.'

'I wondered why we hadn't seen you, so you must be working away.'

'Yes and I get so lonely.'

'Can we come and visit you and cheer you up?'

'It could be dangerous for you and you will have to come at night.'

'Perfect.' said, Bertram. 'Henry will be asleep.'

Mitch who was listening to the conversation said, 'Can I come?'

'Why not.' said Bruce.

'Are you sure about this Mitch, you have very short legs.'

'Yes I know but I don't want to be left all alone at night. Sometimes it can be very spooky in the dark.'

'What in Henry's bedroom, it must be your imagination.'

'No not really – I hear noises in the night.'

'That's Henry snoring.'

'That's settled.' said Bertram and he added 'We can talk about a plan of sorting out Pinch and Punch.'

'Where do you work?'

'It's six houses down from the junction of this road on the left and you won't even have to cross the road. You must be able to see it from the window.'

Bruce went for a run around the garden and he felt happy to think sometime during next week he was going to get someone he could talk to.

Bertram looked across the gardens to the right and saw a roof of a large building in the grounds that backed against the woods that he, Thomas the cat, Al the Owl, George the dog had entered and they had met Peregrine the Falcon who joined them to look for Al's parents. Peregrine had lost his parents too.

Bertram remembered that day especially because he had turned into a boy, but as soon as he came back into the garden he turned into a Bear again.

Bertram was in a dream world and he had heard Henry's bedroom door being opened and it was too late to get back to the shelf.

'What on earth are you doing on that window ledge – I'm beginning to think that you can walk.'

Bertram's hard glazed eyes stared back at his owner as Thomas liked to call her. She gently placed him next to Mitch who seemed to be laying flat on his face. She picked him up and gave him a cuddle and said, 'You were my little bear when I was a young girl. I couldn't give you away like the other toys I had.' She placed him on the shelf next to Bertram and then she picked him up again and gave him another long cuddle and then kissed him on the forehead.

She made Henry's bed and left the room. Mitch was crying.

Chapter 6 Visiting Hours

Sunday soon passed and Henry was off to school again. He seemed to be busy writing out a long message. Thomas was able to inform Bertram and Mitch that it was the School outing on Saturday according to Henry's mum who read out what Henry had written about the visit to a Museum. Thomas said that she had read it to him personally and it must have been because the Tony left the room as soon as she started to read it out. He said something about peace and quiet as he went out of the room.

*　　　　　*　　　　　*　　　　　*

It never dawned on Bertram and Mitch on how they were going to get out of the house, let alone get back in and if Henry awoke suddenly would they be far away enough not to have worried about this happening. But then again if they were out of his range they would be safe, but then again if and when they came back and if for some reason he was awake they would turn back to being just teddy bears abandoned.

Bertram had a brilliant idea on how they were going to visit Bruce, so climbing down the drainpipe to the ground they walked down the garden and into the woods and Bertram changed into a boy and he picked up Mitch and went to visit Bruce.

Bertram climbed over a fence clutching Mitch in one hand and Bruce was waiting.

He said, 'Is that...that you Bertram...you look different?'

'It's me,' said Bertram. 'I've changed a little bit, but it was the only way we could get here.'

Bertram told Bruce all about Al the Owl who had got separated from his parents and what happened to him when he walked into the woods. It was far too soon and it was beginning to get lighter and the birds in the trees beyond the yard were beginning to chirp and it was time that Bertram and Mitch left and they went back the way that they had come. On the edge of the woods they stopped suddenly at the unexpected spectacle. Henry was hanging out of his window shouting out 'Who's stolen my bears?'

'Oh...oh!' said, Mitch. 'What shall we do now?'

'I haven't the faintest idea.' said Bertram.

It was a waiting game as Bertram and Mitch sat down on a stump of a tree hoping Henry hadn't been heard or had fallen asleep. No chance as the light went on in Henry's bedroom and the chief and Henry's mum ran into the room.

Both Bertram and Mitch fell asleep, it had been a tiring night. When they awoke everything was eerily quiet and Bertram ventured with Mitch in his arms up the garden towards the house and then they both turned into teddy bears and Henry pointed towards them.

'Look!' he said, 'My teddy bears – I bet those cats next door tried to steal them.'

Linda went down the stairs and picked up Bertram and Mitch and noted with alarm that Bertram's expression had changed slightly, he was actually smiling.

Chapter 7 Thomas

Linda said, 'There is something funny going on, every time I pick up that bear.' She pointed to Bertram he has a different expression on his face.'

Tony said, 'You must be imagining all this and besides when I was a little boy I had Bertram and every time I picked him up he looked different and my mother always said little boys and girls live in their own world and believe what they want to believe.

'Did you believe your mother?'

'Yes and no.'

'What kind of answer is that?'

'Well! It was my world and when I wished my bear to be glad he smiled and when I wanted him to be sad, he looked glum. It's such a long time ago, I can't really remember and it's no good asking Henry I don't think he looks at Bertram in the same way.

'Do you think I'm doing the right thing, I mean buying this new bear for Henry this Christmas?' said Linda.

'What does it do?'

'Everything you don't expect a toy bear would do - It walks and talks.'

Henry's mum and dad left the bedroom.

Bertram felt a jolt that rippled through his whole being, another Bear. Bertram felt that his days were numbered and he couldn't show himself to Henry or his mother and father because they would think it was some kind of witchcraft. He needed to bide his time and a thought had come into his head like a lamp bulb.

Thomas came into Henry's bedroom and although he still had scars from his fight with Punch, he was able to nimbly spring onto Henry's bed and onto the shelf next to Bertram.

Thomas said, 'Have you heard the news about Henry's new Christmas present?'

'Yes just now.'

'How are you going to cope?'

'After the shock of hearing that there is going to be the patter of new feet walking across Henry's bedroom floor, I have come to the conclusion to accept the situation and think of a plan to sort things out.'

Thomas said, 'That's fighting talk and also the best way to tackle the problem ahead and anyway you will have another shock when you see the bear.'

'What about the bear?'

'It's the spitting image of you and the same size complete with scarf.'

'That makes things a lot easier doesn't it.'

'How come?'

'I can take over and go for walks and talk.'

'It can only happen when Henry goes to sleep or goes to school.'

'Oh yes! I forgot – it doesn't matter at the moment, what are going to do with the menaces next door?'

'I was hoping you would know.'

'Don't worry Thomas I'll think of something.'

Chapter 8 Pinch and Punch

Punch said in pussy language to Pinch, 'I don't really know what the fuss is all about and why are we not talking like those next door?'

'Don't ask me?' said, Pinch.

'This is most peculiar.'

'You can say that again.'

'I won't.'

'You know what I mean.'

'Yes! I know what you mean.'

Punch was confined to the house because the owner next door complained about the injuries that Thomas sustained from his unprovoked attack – whatever that meant. Pinch was a visitor to his estranged brother.

'Tell you what, why don't you pretend to be me and trot downstairs and see how the land lies.'

'I suppose I could, but they might check to see if it was you.'

'You'll have to take that chance and anyway they have to lift your tail to see that different mark and if you swish it round like I do, they won't bother.'

Punch goes off swishing his tail to the right and then to the left, it reminded him of the car he rode in on the way to his doctor, these things kept going backwards and forwards over the glass, he noted it only happened when it rained. He was fascinated by their movement and he crouched in his commando mode and wriggled his bottom as if to pounce and then realised he was in a cage.

He walks into the kitchen and goes straight to Punch's bowl and eats the food and laps up some milk. He has his back to the owner and they don't see the grimace on his face as he hates Pinch's food and he never drinks milk. But a puss has to do what a puss has......he couldn't quite remember what a puss should do and it wasn't a priority. He sauntered outside in the garden and looked up at the window and saw Pinch looking out and gave him an equivalent thumbs up with his tail.

He sprang up the fence that seemed to be in the way as he had not seen the dug-out hole at the bottom. Thomas was half in and half out of a makeshift house being talked to by George who seemed to be doing some exercises and Punch heard the tail end of what he was saying.........'and that's how you fling your opponent to the ground.'

Punch moved towards them and George seeing the cat made to move towards him to protect Thomas . Thomas held his injured paw in front of George to stop him and not to make trouble.

Punch stopped in his tracks and sat down as George moved towards him. Thomas beckoned Punch over by raising his head up in the air and down towards the ground and Punch got up slowly and walked towards them not knowing how things were going to turn out.

It turned out okay. Punch apologised for hurting Thomas and Thomas said he was sorry to have bitten Punch's ear. Punch said that was okay as it matched the other ear.

The talking came to an abrupt end when a voice yelled out from over the fence.

'Punch you come here this minute, you naughty boy, you disobeyed me by going out. Poor old Pinch you tied him up with some wool.' Punch jumped onto the fence and down on the ground and looked up with such an innocent look on his face – he scampered smartly through his cat flap – ate a bit of cat-food and then shot off upstairs to the room. He cowered when the owner caught up with him and tried to hide under a book-case. It was too small for him to get under. 'Come here you silly cat.' She stooped and picked him up and cuddled him and kissed his forehead – he purred. She said, 'I hope you apologised to Thomas for your rough behaviour.'

Obviously he couldn't tell her he had. The owner left the room and Punch turned to look at Pinch.

'What went wrong?'

'I didn't know she was going to lift my tail.'

Chapter 9 What are we going to do?

Henry had gone to School and Bertram and Mitch had come to life and a meeting had been set up as soon as the Linda had gone shopping and the Tony had gone to work. It was a long time since Bertram and Mitch used the stairs and they decided to travel down by the banister route, it was easy and quicker and as long as you got off before you reached the post at the end, you would be okay.

It was a brilliant day – the sun was shining and not a cloud in the sky and surprising enough Pinch and Punch were attending the meeting, apparently Thomas had invited them along stating more heads are better than.............he couldn't remember the saying.

Bertram was glad he hadn't intervened when a fight broke out in the garden between Thomas and Punch and although poor Thomas had come off worse, all had been patched up between them.

A new threat had appeared in the neighbourhood when the people that had moved with Bruce, Pinch and Punch and their family had decided to move away for personal reasons that hadn't been discussed openly. The new people were different and the three children were noisy and naughty. Bruce kept guard over the weekend when his master hastily built the dividing fence and it was understood that hostile forces were now imminent and the meeting of animals and Bertram and Mitch in Henry's garden was to discuss ways and means of defending themselves. Bertram had been made Chairperson and Mitch the Secretary. It was going to be a difficult time because none of the members could write down what they had discussed.

It was a sight to see two stuffed bears, three cats and two dogs sitting in a circle and they looked as if they were talking to each other when the owner of George came out in the garden to hang out the washing. The puzzled look on her face as with a basin of washing and a peg bag she walked down the garden to where the clothes line was and looking back at the circle there seemed to be either quiet barking and meowing and she thought she could see the bears moving their mouths, but that was ridiculous. I must be elucidating – she shook her head and bent down to pick up the first bit of clothing and glanced sideways as she pegged it to the line. There was nobody to be seen excepting George who was gnawing a bone half in and half out of his kennel. She muttered to herself. 'How stupid of me I must have been dreaming.'

Had she looked over the fence, she might have changed her mind as Bruce was giving Bertram and Mitch a ride on his back and he pushed the back door open and trotted upstairs to Henry's bedroom. He just managed to get out of the house without being seen as Thomas owner came in with the shopping.

Chapter 10 Bertram Bear Lookalike

Christmas Day was just 70 days away and Bertram was wondering how he was going to cope with the pressure, knowing that his lookalike was going to be part of Henry's family and more than likely he will be left on the shelf and abandoned and maybe sent to second had shop to be sold on to help a charity in need. He didn't mind helping other persons in their hour of need, but not by losing the family he loved being with, after all wasn't he the one that rescued Henry's mother wedding ring.

He dived just like a goalie and caught it in mid-flight and landed in a bush.

*   *   *   *

Excited voices from below as Linda came back from her shopping with a large parcel under her arm. Bertram Bear could not resist climbing down from the shelf and out on the landing and looking down through the posts of the banister – she was hanging her coat and hat up and she shouted to the man of the house who had come home early. 'I've got it – I had to queue and it was a long queue, I am sorry to be so late, everybody must be getting a Bertram Bear this Christmas.' The chief person said, 'We had better hide it away before Henry comes home from school.'

'I'll put it in the airing cupboard for now, Henry won't look in there.'

'Pity you didn't leave it wrapped up.'

'I would have done, but they told me in the shop to open the parcel and check that everything was as it should be including the two keys.'

'Ah!' murmured Tony.

Henry's mum looked at her watch.

'No time to wrap it now, Henry will be coming through that door in ten minutes time.'

Bertram Bear had forgotten where he was and Linda was coming up the stairs and he wasn't aware until she was nearly level with him and he made a mad dash into Henry's bedroom and scrambled up the bed and onto the shelf.

Henry's mum came rushing into the bedroom and looked up at the shelf. Bertram Bear was there and had that stony stare. She walked out of the room shaking her head and said to herself, 'I must be seeing things, I thought I saw the bear on the landing.'

At that moment the front door opened with force as it swung back on its hinges and hit the wall and the doorknob had made a nice dent in the wall as the door having been opened violently as Henry came home since his school days started.

His father always said, 'I wish you wouldn't do that Henry?'

Henry always answered, 'Sorry Dad.' Linda hastily put the bear

in the airing cupboard and wandered back into Henry's room.

Bertram Bear was sitting on the window ledge swinging his legs backwards and forwards and he spoke 'Why did you buy that Bear?'

Henry mum shrieked loudly and fainted. Henry and his dad came rushing into the bedroom.

Chapter 11   Trick or Treat!

Bertram Bear wondered why he had scared Henry's mum like that and also couldn't understand why it was possible to be able to do things with Henry home from school. It was a revelation of some sort and perhaps now that there was a possibility of being replaced by a wind-up bear, the writing was on the wall for Bertram. It was hard for Bertram to have that stony look when Henry and Tony rushed into Henry's bedroom. Bertram had just managed to scramble back onto the shelf. Linda was starting to come round and she looked up at the shelf and pointed and blabbed something incoherent. Both Henry and Tony looked up, but saw nothing out of place, just the two bears staring into space.

Tony took Linda to their bedroom and came back to Henry's bedroom to pick up keys and other things that had fallen out of Linda's pocket.

Henry took a second glance at Bertram and it looked as if the bear was looking down and grinning. Henry murmured, 'He can't be!'

'What did you say Henry?'

'The bear he was looking down.'

'It's your imagination Henry. I used to think he could do anything I asked.' His dad added and pointed to Bertram. 'He was my bear when I was young, he used to ride a horse and become Lancelot, a policeman on horseback and all sorts of things.'

'Is he sort of magic?'

'No. Not really, he was just my best friend and I used to cuddle him and come to think of it, I haven't had a cuddle for ages.'

Tony took Bertram in his arms and had a long cuddle. Bertram became emotional and a tear began to form in his eye as he rested his chin on master's shoulder and Henry took a step backwards in amazement as his dad turned into a little boy again and disappeared from the room.

*   *   *   *

It was as if a window had been opened and there was a swirl of air rushing round the room. Henry was having this wild dream. He was sprawled in a small bed. It wasn't his room and his mum and dad were looking down at him. He wasn't able to speak and what came from his mouth was "Ga - ga – ga!" His head jerked from side to side and he panicked as he saw the wooden struts each side of him. He thought he was in prison.

*   *   *   *

The little boy looked puzzled. He was in the garden of a house he didn't recognise. The sun was shining with a slight summer breeze wafting across the garden.

There was a blanket spread on the ground. His mother was preparing his tea. He remembered it was his birthday and as a special treat she said they would have tea in the garden. There were small cut sandwiches and lots of assorted cakes, some with icing on top and some filled with chocolate and cream. He was cuddling a big bear that he received. It was his main birthday present. His mother said, 'Anthony, put the bear down and have some sandwiches?'

*　　　　　　*　　　　　　*　　　　　　*

There was a swirl of wind that seemed to be visible as it went round the room and the little boy with the bear in his arms turned back into a man and the man replaced Bertram back on the shelf. He turned to speak to his son, 'That brought back memories of when I was a little boy and somehow I thought I was back in that garden. Perhaps my mind was playing a trick on me.' No one answered, Henry had fallen asleep.

Chapter 12 A Bit of a Wind-up!

It must have been an out of the body experience for both Henry and his dad. His dad was trying to explain to his wife that when he picked up Bertram for a cuddle he seemed to go back in time when he was a little boy and having a picnic in the garden and remembering the precious present he had received from his parents on his birthday.

'I felt I was actually back in that garden.'

'Oh don't be silly.'

'I'm not being silly, I am telling you what I felt.'

'That can't be right.'

'It all brought everything back to me and I remember that day, it was very warm and we had cucumber and beetroot sandwiches and lots of cream cakes. Dad wasn't there at that time. He had been wounded in the war and was in a wheelchair.'

'That reminds me your mum and dad will be visiting us this weekend.'

'You're not listening to what I am saying.'

'I am but I thought I would tell you before I forgot to tell you.'

'It all comes back to me now, dad wheeled himself out into the garden with my birthday cake on his lap and it had different coloured candles on it and I had to blow them all out in one go.'

'Did you?'

'I can't remember. But I'll tell what I did enjoy myself that day. I must cuddle Bertram more often.'

As usual Bertram was being nosey and had been listening to their conversation with interest.

'About time he remembered I was his bear, but really bad timing on his part, what with the other bear and the problem with the new neighbour's animals that we've yet to meet.'

Lunchtime came and everyone sat down to their food, including the animals and then Henry's mum and dad went out again to do some more Christmas shopping.

It was time to open the airing cupboard and take out the Bear, wind it up and see what it could do. It walked okay but the language was very strange. Thomas, Mitch and Bertram couldn't understand a word.

'I can't see me impersonating the Bear and talking that gibberish,' said Bertram.

'Thomas said, 'Perhaps you can change it, there usually is something you can switch.'

'How do you know?'

Thomas said, 'I look at a lot of television and sometimes it's very interesting and I like watching other animals and once there was a programme about cats...........'

Bertram cut Thomas's flow of words, 'That might be very interesting for you, but how do we change this voice?'

'It sometimes can be found under a flap either in the neck or near the bottom.'

'How undignified!' said Bertram. He added, 'Nobody's going to touch my bottom.'

Thomas noted that the time was getting near to the Glovers coming home from their shopping spree and Henry would be home shortly after.

Thomas said, 'We haven't got any more time to fiddle with the bear they will be home shortly.

Bertram just managed to get the toy bear back in the box and into the cupboard when they heard the front door key being used to open the door. Bertram quietly closed the door and scampered with Mitch by his side into Henry's room.

Thomas followed and sat on the window ledge and whispered to the bears Linda and Tony were going shopping again in the morning. There was no time to answer as Linda Glover walked into the room and looked at Bertram and Mitch. She grunted and went out and opened the airing cupboard and took out the bear and took it into her bedroom.

Thomas had turned around and had watched.

He said, 'I think we have another problem.'

'Bertram said, 'What's that?'

'She's taken the bear into her bedroom and if she puts it in her wardrobe on the top shelf, we won't be able to get it.'

Thomas jumped off the window ledge and walked gracefully out of Henry's bedroom. His head reappeared suddenly. 'I have an idea, see you tomorrow chaps.'

Bertram and Mitch wondered what the idea would be.

Bertram said, 'Probably something dramatically dangerous.'

Mitch said, 'I wish you hadn't said that!'

Chapter 13 Bear Hunting

The normal rushing around as Henry prepared to get ready for school, the banging of doors with toothbrush in mouth and then discarded in the usual manner flung back towards the bathroom to be picked up later by his mum. As soon as the front door slammed shut, there was an eerie silence. Each morning a tornado had rushed through the house called Henry. Clothes slung everywhere and a half eaten breakfast and a cold water tap still running and filling the wash basin and every morning his mum went round and turned off, picked up, washed up and tidied.

Henry couldn't get used to the early hour he had to get up to go to his new school and he promised his mum he would get up early the next day, but it never happened.

Whether it was a magic spell or something Bertram was aware of the turmoil and the devastation that Henry left in his slipstream and it was hard to keep that stony eyed stare every time Henry came into the room to pick up last minute items he needed for school. Henry always said goodbye to Bertram before he went to school and it was hard for Bertram not to return the compliment.

The morning returned to normality and Bertram and Mitch heard the clutter of plates being placed in this machine. Breakfast was over for the parents and soon they would be off to do more Christmas shopping, something usually Bertram looked forward to, but not today as they were going Bear hunting and it meant a visit to another room that they hadn't been to before.

Hearing the door close and the car move away, Bertram and Mitch climbed down from the shelf and walked to the landing. Thomas was there with string and two pieces of wood.

Bertram said, 'What's the wood for?'

'I don't know. I just thought they might be useful.'

They walked towards the bedroom and pushed open the door. Bertram blinked as he looked round the room, it was a dull yellow colour. There was a chair with a pair of trousers over the back and some other clothing on the seat.

Thomas said, 'We will want the chair and we will have to push it towards that big cupboard over there.' He pointed with his right paw.

Bertram looked uncertain whether could move the chair and he decided to remove the trousers and other clothing from the chair to make it easier. It wasn't helpful at all but eventually Bertram and Mitch got the chair in front of the big piece of furniture. Thomas managed to hook his paw round a door and it swung open.

Thomas padded off and came back with the string and then went back for one piece of wood and then another piece.

He said to Bertram, 'Can you see if I have a splinter in my mouth, it feels strange?'

Bertram looked at Thomas's mouth and he saw a piece of something sticking out at the corner of it.

'I can't pull it out!' Bertram held out his bunched pads to show why. 'But I have an idea.' He rushed out of the bedroom and into Henry's and shouted out to George to come and help. George was in his usual place – half in and half out of his kennel gnawing a bone. Bertram muttered, 'He's always gnawing a bone.'

George eventually came running in and skidding on the rug in the kitchen and gliding across the floor in a stately manner until he reached the door, narrowly missing a bashed head. He scrambled up the stairs where Bertram was waiting for him.'

'What's the problem?'

Bertram said, 'Can you take out a splinter from Thomas's mouth?'

'What with may I ask?'

'Use your teeth.'

'I suppose I can.'

'Go on, then!'

George said to Thomas, 'Don't think I am getting too personal, but I need to get close to you to do this.'

Thomas didn't answer but closed his eyes tightly and he felt George's breathe on his face as George bit the end of the wood and tugged at it and it came away after the second pull. George moved away and opened his mouth and the offending piece of splinter of wood fell to the floor and George using his nose pushed it under the bed. Thomas was grateful and told George how wonderful he was.

George was curious and wondered what they were up to. Bertram said, 'We have to reach that box on the top shelf and look inside.'

'Why?' said George.

'It's the new Bertram Bear lookalike that Henry's getting for Christmas.'

'Well I can't see how that would make any difference to you....oh yes I see, how awkward.'

'It's more than awkward. I could be made redundant.'

Thomas said, 'This is not getting us any nearer to our problem, we must act now before they come back.'

With the string in his mouth Thomas jumped on the bed and then leapt to the top of the cupboard. Unfurling the string over the door he told Bertram to tie the end round his middle. It was a difficult process with pads for hands but eventually he managed and Thomas pulled Bertram up until he reached the top of the door and somehow Bertram swung into the top shelf. Opening the box and getting the new bear out of the box to have a closer look when they heard the front door open. Bertram dropped the bear and almost clobbered Mitch.

'What shall we do now?' said Thomas.

'I'll climb into the box and you take the other bear and put him on the shelf in Henry's room.'

The only snag was they had forgotten to untie the string round Bertram's middle and had to leave everything where it was. Mitch, Thomas and George dragged the lookalike bear to Henry's bedroom and with much grunting and groaning got him to sit on the shelf. George and Thomas hid under Henry's bed as the lady of the house appeared in Henry's bedroom. She looked at the shelf and then walked into her bedroom. The shock of seeing the room in a state she called down to her man, 'Tony I think we have had burglars.'

Thomas and George heard the noise on the stairs as the man rushed up and into the bedroom.

He asked, 'Anything taken?'

'I don't know, but it doesn't look like it.'

'Perhaps we disturbed them before they could take anything.'

'Do you think there was more than one person?'

'I don't know dear – just check everything.'

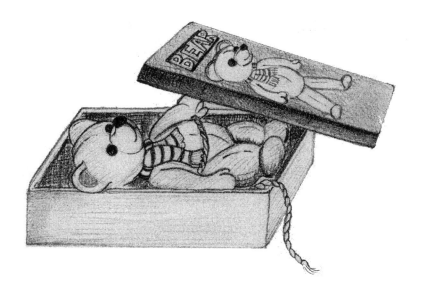

Linda walked to the wardrobe and took down the box and opened it up and the relief on her face was short-lived when she saw the string round Bertram's middle.

'What's this around the middle?'

Tony came to her side, 'Wasn't it there before?'

Linda said, 'No! It wasn't and also the key is missing to wind him up.'

'Did you check to see if it was when you first opened up the box?'

'Yes! Of course I did.'

'Perhaps it dropped out of the box and is in the airing cupboard.'

On hearing this Thomas crawled out from under the bed and leapt up to the shelf and took the key out of the lookalike bear and out onto the landing. Hooking his paw round the door it clicked on the ball-bearing shutting device which was loose and nosed the key inside and with his bottom he leaned against the door and it shut. He ran back and under Henry's bed again.

Linda Glover talking as she walked towards the airing cupboard, 'I don't think I dropped it?' But there it was, just lying inside the door. She walked back and said to her man, 'You were right, it was there. But I still don't understand. Perhaps I'll wind him up and see what he does?'

Bertram Bear flinched and froze in the box as did Mitch, Thomas and George. They were all saved by the front door crashing open and Henry had come home.

Chapter 14　　How to get out of a difficult situation

George and Thomas left Henry's bedroom and made their way to the garden. Tony Glover cleared up the mess in the room and decided not to ring for the police. Linda went down to see how Henry got on at school. She was shocked to find him in the state he was in. He was covered with a good deal of mud and covered with leaves. Henry explained to his mum that to join this special fraternity at school he had to be initiated with a dare and he chose the mud bath. Henry was frog marched to his bedroom and told to strip off – she gave his school uniform to his dad and asked him to clean off the excess of mud and then put it in another machine for washing. She took him into the bathroom and ran the hot and cold taps and stayed and watched him clean himself. It was an opportune moment to switch bears.

Mitch yelled out of Henry's bedroom window that he needed George and Thomas to switch the bears over. Mitch managed to push the lookalike off the shelf and George and Thomas came galloping up the stairs and dragged the lookalike to the other bedroom. Unbeknown to them Henry's dad was sitting on the bed facing the wardrobe with Bertram Bear in his hands.

He muttered to himself, 'I can't see where the key goes to wind him up.'

It was a sticky situation as Mitch, George and Thomas with this bear were stuck in the middle of the bedroom floor. Mitch took the initiative by saying if we sidle up to this side of the bed and keep still he might not notice us. The man laid down Bertram on the bed and went off with the key to the bathroom. Bertram appeared suddenly by the side of the bed and they hoisted up the lookalike and placed him where the man had left Bertram. They just managed to get to the bedroom door as the Glovers came in and picked up the bear and said, 'The key goes in here.' She stuck it into the bear and placed the bear back in the box and put it on the top shelf of the wardrobe and went straight to the bathroom to see how Henry was getting on. The man went downstairs and Mitch, Thomas, George and Bertram went to Henry's room. George was escorted by Thomas downstairs and out of the house and Bertram and Mitch climbed wearily onto the shelf.

Bertram said, 'A fat lot of good that was – we never got to see what the bear could do and if Thomas comes up with another idea, I think we'll ignore it.'

Mitch said, 'You must admit it was fun – all that cloak and dagger stuff we went through. What an adventure, we must do something like that again.'

Bertram just looked at Mitch but said nothing.

Chapter 15   A short Adventure

November had passed and the count down to Christmas day was looming up fast and the Glovers had already put up most of their decorations and even Bertram and Mitch had a small piece of tinsel wrapped round their necks. Henry tried to put some decorations on Thomas, but he was able to shake it all off.

Henry would be having his Winter holiday soon and there didn't seem to be any more opportunities in getting hold of Henry's present to find out what it could do so really Bertram was resigning himself to the prospect of having to wait until Christmas day, had it not been for Henry having such an inquisitive mind and almost ransacked his parent's wardrobe. This had to be blamed on his dad who let slip that his present was somewhere in the house and he would have to wait till Christmas Day. Henry brings the bear into his bedroom and he was disappointed when he opened the box to find another Bertram Bear, even though he knew there was a key and he could wind the bear up and he would walk, do somersaults and talk. To Henry the talking part didn't make any sense. Henry spoke to the new toy 'What is your name?'

'What is your name?' it said.

'Your name is Bertram number two.'

'Your name is Bertram number too.'

'This is silly.'

'This is silly.'

Henry turns off the bear and places him next to Bertram – they were exactly the same. There were instructions that came with the bear, but they were still in the box. Henry went and opened the box which he had left on his parent's bed and tried to read the instructions.

Tony had to confess to his wife that owing to a slip he had more or less told Henry that his Christmas present was in the house and Henry got hold of it and was playing with it in his bedroom.

Henry came down and said, 'What's for tea mum?'

Normally Henry would be bubbling over with excitement every time he had a new present, but not this time.

'What's the matter Henry?' said his dad.

'That bear you bought me, it's stupid. Every time I speak a sentence, it repeats back the same words.'

'I think you have to train it to speak.'

'What do you mean – train it?'

'If you remember your first hand held gadget where you had to keep some pet alive by feeding it every day and teaching it to talk – you'll just have to read the instructions.'

'I would have but the instructions are in a different language.'

'All instruction manuals have different languages and the English one are usually printed at the back of the book and probably the bear was made in China.'

Henry was confused. He decided to have his breakfast before tackling the job of training the lookalike Bertram Bear.

*   *   *   *

'Fancy letting him know we had his Christmas present, honestly.'

'Sorry darling.'

'We'll get him some small presents and hang them on the Christmas tree.'

'How much was that bear?'

'I think it's worth £149.99. My friend Stella got one earlier this year and she is having great fun with it.'

'Is Stella the friend that hasn't any children?'

'Yes and now it is fully trained, it's good company. Just like a friend with no complications.'

*   *   *   *

Henry rushed upstairs and looked up at the bears and he couldn't remember which bear was the one that you wind up and which one was his favourite Bertram. He remembered he didn't have to wind it up, he had done that before breakfast. He took the bear down and sat it on the bed. He touched the back of it and it said, 'My name is Bertram Bear.'

Henry was overcome with awe. He read the pamphlet a little bit more and said, 'How old are you?' The bear was silent for a moment and then it said, 'I am two years old – how old are you?'

Henry was stunned and he rushed out of the bedroom and down the stairs and into the kitchen where his parents were still having their breakfast.

Henry shouted, 'It's a marvelous toy, it's already spoken back to me.'

'That was quick.' His dad said.

Mum said, 'Perhaps we could have it back and give it to you on Christmas day. It won't be long before we reach the 25th.'

Mum didn't hold out much hope but was surprised when Henry said, 'Okay mum – I'll go and get the bear.'

*   *   *   *

'That was good said Bertram Bear, being able to speak to Henry without him knowing.

Thomas walked into the bedroom and said, 'You better climb back on the shelf as you will be put away in a box until Christmas day.'

Mitch knocked the other bear off the shelf and Bertram caught it and placed it on the bed and managed to get on the shelf as Henry grabbed hold of the lookalike and rushed out and downstairs.

His mum brought the bear upstairs and walked into Henry's bedroom, she wasn't sure about Bertram ever since that time…… her thoughts dwindled………how silly of me. She walked out of the room into her bedroom and placed the bear into the box and put it in her wardrobe and gently closed the door.

Chapter 16   What Shall We Do?

Bertram had quite forgotten about the other problem that seemed to dwarf his own personal one with the lookalike bear as he liked to call it and it wasn't until Charlie the Hedgehog appeared in the garden that the full horrific was revealed.

Charlie was suffering having been harassed by large dog that kept sniffing at him and then being pushed along and it wasn't until Charlie rolled himself up in a neat little ball, so that he showed all of his needle sharp spikes was he considered safe, even though he was unable to move.

The dog that had attacked him hadn't learnt his lesson and received a nasty sting on his nose and ran off yelping. Charlie seized the moment and ran as fast as he could to the fence and was under it and through to the next garden. Charlie came face to face with Bruce and his heart almost stopped. Bruce said, 'It's okay. You know need to fear me. I'll escort you to Thomas's garden.'

Charlie entered the garden in the usual manner under the fence. There seemed to be a lot of noise from the garden where Charlie had escaped from the dog, which nobody could determine what breed it was hung his paws over the top of the fence, his mouth open with all his teeth showing and making the most horrifying noise and looking straight at Bruce, who stood his ground, bared his teeth and snarled back. It might have been a different story had there been no fence between them.

Charlie was telling his story and after he finished he asked Thomas if he could have his usual hot milk and bread. Charlie managed a rasping cough. Thomas though that his Linda should have another look at Charlie in case he had suffered some sort of injury. It was with soft tender hands that she picked up Charlie and examined him. There was no injuries but she felt that Charlie was slightly traumatised and made up a box with a piece of towel and placed him near the kitchen stove.

Bertram had been watching from Henry's bedroom window and had slid down the drainpipe to join Thomas and he said, 'We ought to call a meeting and discuss a plan of how we are going to tame this brute.'

Thomas said, 'Tame him! Have you seen the size of him?'

'However big he is we'll have to do something.'

Thomas said, 'What about the cats. I understand there are three of them and if their names are anything to go by – we will have a fight on our hands.'

'What names have they got?'

'Biff, Bash and Butt.'

'Quaint!' said, Bertram.

'We will have to do something, that's for sure.'

'I think I better go for a walk in the woods and get help.'

'What kind of help can you get in the woods?'

'You'll see.' said, Bertram.

'If I go tomorrow morning George will be able to accompany me. In the meantime if you get the rest of the gang ready for a meeting and don't forget to ask Pinch and Punch.'

Thomas said, 'Okay!'

Chapter 17   Enter Biff, Bash and Butt

The following morning Bertram prepared himself for his epic journey. The walk from the rear of the house to the bottom of the garden was going to be slow for a bear. But when he became a boy he would be able to stride out.

George made sure he had a hefty breakfast and took along a small bone to chew on should he get pangs of hunger.

Bertram knew who he wanted to see in the woods and he was hopeful that they hadn't moved away. The woods seemed a lot denser since the last time he had come and it seemed ages before they came across the tree-home of Mr and Mrs Owl and their son Al. Pleasantries were passed between them and each were glad to have a natter about what happened since last time they were together. Bertram put across this plan and to succeed he needed their help and could Mr. Owl try and find Peregrine and his mum and dad. It was a tall order for Mr. Owl, but he said he would try.

Bertram and George said their goodbyes.

Bertram said, 'I wonder what the time is?'

George replied, 'About one pm.'

'How do you know that?'

George stopped and stood up and leaning against a tree and with one paw he rubbed his stomach. 'I'm hungry.'

'We will soon be back but if you like George you run off home and get something to eat.'

George said, 'Are you sure you will be okay?'

'Yes, you carry on.'

George went off at great speed and as Bertram was nearing the edge of the wood and the beginning of the garden George came back.

'I don't like to say this, but something awful has happened and things are worsening.'

'What has happened?'

Bertram had already passed the threshold into the garden and had turned back into a bear. He could see the danger and ran as fast as his short bear legs allowed and hid inside the shed and peered through the window as three cats searched the garden looking for things to damage and Bertram witnessed Thomas on his hind legs trying to defend himself against two of them and at the first opportunity he ran like the wind and through the cat flap and upstairs. One of the cats entered but was quickly escorted out of the house by Tony. The cats got together and searched the whole area of the garden.

They neared the shed door which Bertram was leaning against hoping that his weight would be enough to stop them if they tried to get in. Thankfully they didn't try the door, probably because Bertram wasn't an animal with a scent that would register in their noses. Eventually after loitering for a further hour they gave up and went home.

Bertram made his way from the shed and back to the house he was trembling with the shock that if those cats had come into the shed, it didn't bear thinking about and as walked he saw how the garden looked. There were many holes in the lawn, small tree branches broken and there was still worse news to come.

Pinch and Punch had been away for a couple of nights hunting in the woods. The owners were aware of this as this had happened many times before where they used to live. They were coming home when they made the mistake of running across the garden as a short cut. Punch had managed to get across safely, but Pinch was caught by the Growler who had his teeth round the blue collar of Pinch and tossed him high in the air and although cats have the ability to land on four feet he unfortunately landed on a piece of concrete with a piece of rust covered spike showing through. Pinch was badly injured and it meant a trip to his doctors for treatment.

Chapter 18   The Plan

Thomas decided the best course of action was to stay in doors while everything quietened down. Why put yourself in danger when you can feel cosy and safe in your home. George was absent from his garden. Bertram and Mitch were watching the sky line every day hoping to see their helpers arrive. A week went by and there was nothing to report. It was on the Saturday when Bertram and Mitch heard the noise of many birds and the branches in the woods bowed down with the weight of them and although the garden was 150 feet in length they could see that their reinforcements had finally arrived and there were much more than they could have imagined. From the woods a large bird emerged and flew effortless towards them – it was Peregrine.

He said, 'Your forces await your orders!

Bertram said, 'I'm sorry but it is too soon. We haven't been able to meet and discuss anything – but I do have a plan.

Peregrine said, 'That's okay then?'

'It comes in two parts and the first part is going to be tricky to perform, because we have to get the scapegoat that is going to give us a chance to spring a surprise on our nasty friends two gardens away.

'Who is going to be the scapegoat?' said, Peregrine.

'Henry's Christmas present.'

'Pardon!' said, Peregrine.

Bertram said, 'I'll explain – Henry received a lookalike Bertram Bear that you wind up – it walks and talks and if we can set it up over their fence and get it to across their lawn, it's bound to attract some attention.'

'Yes I can see the reason for that. But what do you want us birds to do?'

'Linda's husband Tony has some netting in the shed and we need to break in and get it and it is essential to my plan. When the lookalike bear is attacked, the birds have to fly over and drop the weighted netting on all four of them, and bobs your uncle.'

'You never said anything about weights.'

'Oh didn't I, it must have slipped my mind.'

'What kind of weights had you in mind?'

'Something that has a handle on it so it's easy to hold like a steam iron.'

'Peregrine said, 'I don't think so – that group of birds won't be strong enough.'

'How many are there?'

'About a hundred and you'll need a thousand.'

'We can't have too many, the noise will give the game away.

'Your plan has a few loop-holes in it.'

'That is why I want to have a meeting to discuss it with George and the rest of the group.'

'In the meantime I will fly off and see if I can get my parents and their friends to come – then I think we will have a chance of winning.'

'Okay – I'll call a meeting for this afternoon in George's garden, we should be safe there.'

'What about Henry's present, he won't be too happy about that.'

'I know and I feel awful about having to use it, but I can't see any other way around the problem. It's just fortunate for us that Henry got his present out early.'

'So why will it be difficult to get at?'

'He gave it back to his mum to look after until Christmas day and that's the problem.'

'Where is it then?'

'Hidden away somewhere in their bedroom.'

'Good luck with that. I better fly off – I have a long way to go and while I'm away think about the weights and how we are going to fix them.'

'No problem there.' said Bertram.

Peregrine flew off with a frown on his face and muttered as he went, 'Who is he going to get to tie the weights on?'

*   *   *   *

It was quite a gathering – Pinch with paw in sling, Punch, Thomas, George, Charlie, Mitch and Bertram. They were assembled in George's garden shed. Bruce was standing guard in his garden and should there be any sign of the four he would bark twice.

Bertram said, 'First item on the agenda. I need Mitch to sacrifice his freedom to exchange with the lookalike me in the box before it is wrapped up.'

'The weight will be different.'

'I know and I have solved that by giving you a book to take with you and that should compensate the weight problem.'

'Supposing Linda opens the box first – what do we do then?'

'We carry on – it's our only chance of success.'

'She will go round the house looking for it.'

'I know and I think the greenhouse will be a great place to hide the bear.'

'Right shall we move on – Thomas it will be your job to get the keys to the shed.'

'What do you want in the shed?'

'I noticed there were bottles with corks in there plus string, scissors and skewers or anything that has a point that can be stuck in the ground and most importantly the garden netting and get all of it.'

Thomas's eyebrows raised slightly. 'How am I going to get all those things out by myself?'

'George, Pinch and Punch will help you once you get in.'

'It's a tall order you have given us.'

'I think you will find some bags that you can put the items in.'

'Where do you want all this stuff to go to?'

'If you can drag it so it is out of sight of the house windows and just inside the woods.'

'That's a long way and it will take time.'

'That's why we'll have to do this at night and the following day will be a Sunday and nobody is up early and that's the day we do it.'

'Charlie, your job is to try and keep Henry's mum busy in the kitchen.

'What shall I do?'

'Do anything you like, look cute or roll up in a ball or if you can go on your back and show your tummy or look pleadingly that you would like some hot milk with bread.'

Thomas said, 'I know this is going to be the wrong sort of question, but what about Henry's dad?'

'When he goes into the shed – lock him in.'

'You don't want much do you?'

'All these things I have thought of are key factors in our campaign and if we want to get rid of these thorns in our sides we have to rise to the occasion.'

Thomas said, 'What will you be doing Bertram?'

'My key role will be filling the bottles with water and then placing on the corks and tying the bottles and skewers to the netting.'

'How are you going to do that with your paws?'

'I shall be doing this in the woods when I turn into a boy.'

Thomas said, 'Oh yes! I forgot about that.'

'One more thing for you and I to do tonight.'

'What is that?'

'We have to find the box with the lookalike Bear and get Mitch to take its place and go and hide it in the greenhouse.'

'What happens in the woods?'

'We wait for the heavy mob to arrive.'

Bruce barked twice and everyone dispersed quickly as they could.

Bertram was going to add what would happen next but they were interrupted.

Chapter 19   Commando Style

Thomas said, 'You don't expect me to black my face, do you?'

Bertram said, 'Well it's up to you, but if you're seen by anyone we'll have to stop.'

'Do you know how difficult it is to clean my fur each day and to put black shoe polish on the owners may think they have another cat in the house, anyway we don't need to do that to get the other bear.

'I suppose not.'

Bertram said, 'We better go and get the box.'

Thomas said, 'That's going to be tricky, Linda has already taken it downstairs.'

'When?' said, Bertram.

'Just now when you were talking about blacking my face with shoe polish.'

'Why didn't you say so!'

Bertram, Thomas and a reluctant Mitch crept downstairs. Both Linda and Tony were in the kitchen making hot drinks for themselves. Thomas was keeping guard as Bertram and Mitch went into the lounge.

Bertram found the box on a table with a few other boxes for wrapping. He prised up the lid and took the lookalike out and Mitch with book he took from the book case in the lounge climbed into the box and Bertram wished him luck and pressed down the lid.

Linda came in as Bertram got off the table and hid under the chair. He waited for the man to come in and then in commando style he crawled towards the door when the lady said, close the door darling it's chilling in here. Bertram got up and ran and it wasn't easy with the lookalike as big as him but he managed to get out by the skin of his fur.

Bertram announced, 'Phase one accomplished.' He nodded to nobody as Thomas was nowhere to be seen.

Phase 2 and 3 were the next step and it was just a matter of getting the keys and taking them off of a hook in the kitchen. They weren't there, they were on the kitchen table and Thomas using his nose pushed them off. The man came in and looked at the table and said, 'That's funny I thought I put them on the table while I was making the drink.' He shrugged his shoulders and added, 'I'll look for them later.'

Getting the keys out of the house, especially through the cat flap was difficult and another problem was getting the key up to that keyhole was another ordeal. Pinch at the bottom with Punch next and then Thomas with key in mouth inserted and turned it sideways to the right. He couldn't go any further and climbed down and asked Bertram to turn it the rest of the way. The three cats got down to getting all the items together and it took ages to get all that was needed to get to the bottom of the garden. The netting was the last item as it was a larger size than they imagined. Bertram helped them and as he thought of all these ideas of what they had to do, wasn't expecting to help in all the jobs that he had farmed out to the group.

Bertram announced, 'Phases two and three were completed.'

There had been many hitches overlooked and the biggest was now facing them. It all sounded feasible when Bertram talked about what they were going to do and especially what he was going to do. It was going to be an all night job to complete phase four of Bertram's idea. Not realising the distance between the water butts round the shed and the greenhouse was going to be the problem. In the woods Bertram would become a boy, in the garden he would become a bear and getting the water wasn't going to be easy unless Bertram came up with another idea. Bertram was full of ideas, but none of them seem to work until another came out of the blue. If he tied two bottles together with string he could place them over the back of George and he could run to one of the butts. Another snag came apparent when he couldn't open the tap at the bottom. Thomas said, 'Hold on I have an idea.' He ran down the garden and into the shed. The noise seemed to be quite deafening but soon he came out with a large screwdriver which he half dragged up the garden.

'What do you hope to do with that?' George said.

'I've seen this done by Henry's dad and it worked for him, so it must work for me if I have the strength.'

'What's that then?'

'If I wedge this screwdriver in the tap and push it round it should open.'

Thomas pushed hard digging his hind legs into the ground and the tap moved and a small trickle of water started to come out. However, there was another snag, the bottle wouldn't go under the tap.

Thomas said, 'What are we going to do now?'

'I have an idea, so don't worry.'

George started to scratch the ground and eventually a hole appeared under the tap and George stood with his flank next to the tap and the water trickled into the bottles. It was an ungainly stand as he had his front and hind legs straddled across the hole and he had to move sideways, so he wouldn't fall in the hole.

He ran off and disappeared into woods and then came back with another two bottles and so on until there were no more bottles to be filled. Thomas's shoulder was sore as he had to put pressure on the tap in an upward stance to keep the water tap open.

Bertram thanked George and Thomas for their heroic deed. Bertram as a boy was able to do his part with ease. He told everyone to get some sleep as in two hours time they would have to start on their final phase which was going to be difficult.

Bertram was the only one who didn't go to sleep as toy bears seldom did. He lay on the ground and watched the moon slide across the sky until clouds blotted it out. Bertram guessed two hours had passed and began to wake up the gang and it was just then a flight of Peregrine Falcons flew over and did a tight circle and gracefully landed by the group. Peregrine came to Bertram and said his mum couldn't come along as she was expecting, but with his wing he pointed to the rest of them, these are all the fathers that are waiting for that special moment. We will see if we can lift the netting as a test and see if we need to make some adjustments. All the birds including the Crows and Jackdaws, who didn't want to be left out of the adventure grabbed a piece of netting and lifted up in the air – it was alright, everything was a go situation. As a boy Bertram walked the rear of the gardens with the lookalike bear with Pinch, Punch, George and Thomas. Their job once the netting had been dropped was to hammer in the skewers into the ground as quickly as possible.

Bertram looked through a hole in the fence and saw the three cats prowling around the garden, but no dog. Bertram wound up the lookalike Bear and opened the door and set the bear to walk fast. It walked and walked and Bertram didn't think the plan was going to work until all three came hurtling towards their target.

Bertram gave the signal and the birds flew over and dropped the netting over them and George and the rest of the team ran towards the netting and striking the skewers with stones they found in the garden deep into the ground. Growler appeared. He was yawning and showing his enormous teeth as he rushed towards George and the rest of them. They stood their ground petrified of what was going to happen to them. It never happened – Bruce seeing the danger leapt over the fence and landed on Growler, knocking him out. Bruce and Bertram's team pulled Growler along the ground until he was under part of the netting and they covered that part with stones. Growler awoke but couldn't move.

All the birds stood silently round the netting showing their talons and Peregrine picking his way over the netting issued a warning to the cats and the dog, 'If you attack our friends or go into their garden we will come back and...........' he left that word unsaid and all the birds showed their talons and one Falcon cut in half a piece of the netting with his claws.

Although unknown to the cats and dog, the netting had already been cut with a pair of scissors by Bertram in the woods. The birds lifted the netting just enough for their quarries to leave. They landed again and followed them back to the house. Their hooded eyes were enough to send shivers down Growlers spine and he spoke to Biff, Bash and Butt, 'If you decide to go after them, you're on your own.'

They all disappeared into their house.

The Falcons picked up the netting and flew back to Bertram's garden and placed the netting near the shed.

Bertram picked up the lookalike bear, he wasn't damaged as much as he first thought. Bruce gave them all a piggy-back ride home, but they had to hold on tightly as he leapt one fence and dropped off Pinch and Punch and then leapt over the fence to Bertram and Thomas's garden. George scrambled under the fence back to his kennel. Bertram thanked Peregrine for getting all his friends to help.

'Any time Bertram, if you need help just go and see Al the Owl – we will come.'

Bertram's legs were sore with so much walking and the thought of having to sort out the netting was too much. Thomas escorted Bertram back to Henry's bedroom. He placed the lookalike on the shelf and sat next to him.

Chapter 20 Christmas Day

Bertram hadn't planned ahead on what to do with clearing up and getting Mitch out of the already parcel that Henry's mum had done yesterday and there would be nobody who could explain the reasons how or why all this upset happened.

Thomas came into the room and said that he and George had managed to get the netting back in the shed but everything was still tied to it. The shed door would be open and the keys to the shed had been replaced on the hook and that would be another mystery.

Bertram thought of a way to get the lookalike bear back, well not exactly in the box, but if he put it behind the Christmas tree and out of sight, it would look like Henry had just got it out of the box, that was the theory. Bertram got of the shelf with the lookalike and he walked downstairs and into the lounge and there in the corner was the Christmas tree all adorned with tinsel lights and baubles – the presents in their packages were under the tree. Bertram knew which parcel it was and was able to tear the paper and lift the lid. Grabbed hold of Mitch and his book and replaced it with the lookalike bear. He managed to place the lid and cover it with the wrapping paper and from a distance it would look wrapped.

Dodging and weaving back to Henry's bedroom was quite a journey and having to hear what happened to Charlie the Hedgehog was an adventure in itself.

Apparently Linda thought Charlie had another injury because when she saw him in the kitchen there was a fork that had fallen off the sink area and had stuck into the lino and Charlie's paw had got in the way – so another visit to the animal hospital. He was having the life of Riley being fed and looked after by Linda while outside everything was happening.

Christmas Day arrived and everybody had a wonderful time and presents were handed out to Pinch, Punch and Bruce and then to George from the Thomas's owner. Thomas got his favourite food and Bertram and Mitch were quite content with life.

What happened to the lookalike Bertram Bear – it was played with a couple of times and then placed in the toy cupboard. When a charity person called round the lookalike bear was given to them for children who haven't any toys.

The End

The next story Bertram Bear Rules!

44036096R00047

Printed in Poland
by Amazon Fulfillment
Poland Sp. z o.o., Wrocław